This Boxer Book belongs to

. . . .

For Isobel and Alasdair

J.A

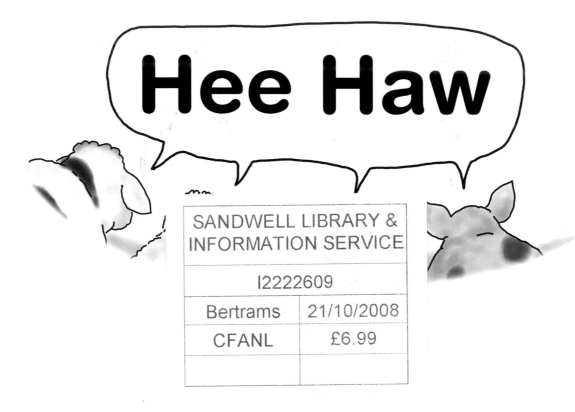

First published in Great Britain in 2008
by Boxer Books Limited.
www.boxerbooks.com

Text and illustrations copyright © 2008 Jonathan Allen

The rights of Jonathan Allen to be identified as the author
and illustrator of this work have been asserted by him
in accordance with the Copyright, Designs and Patents Act, 1988.

ISBN 13: 978-1-905417-80-3

1 3 5 7 9 10 8 6 4 2

Printed in China

The Little Rabbit Who Liked to Say MOO

Jonathan Allen

Boxer Books

Little Rabbit sat in the farmer's field.

"Moo," said Little Rabbit. "Moo."

"Why are you saying moo?" asked Calf.

"You're not a cow."

"I like moo," said Little Rabbit,

"and rabbits don't have a big noise."

"Can you make other noises?"
asked Calf.

"I like baa," said Little Rabbit.

"So do I," said Calf.

Little Rabbit and Calf made the biggest "baaa" they could.

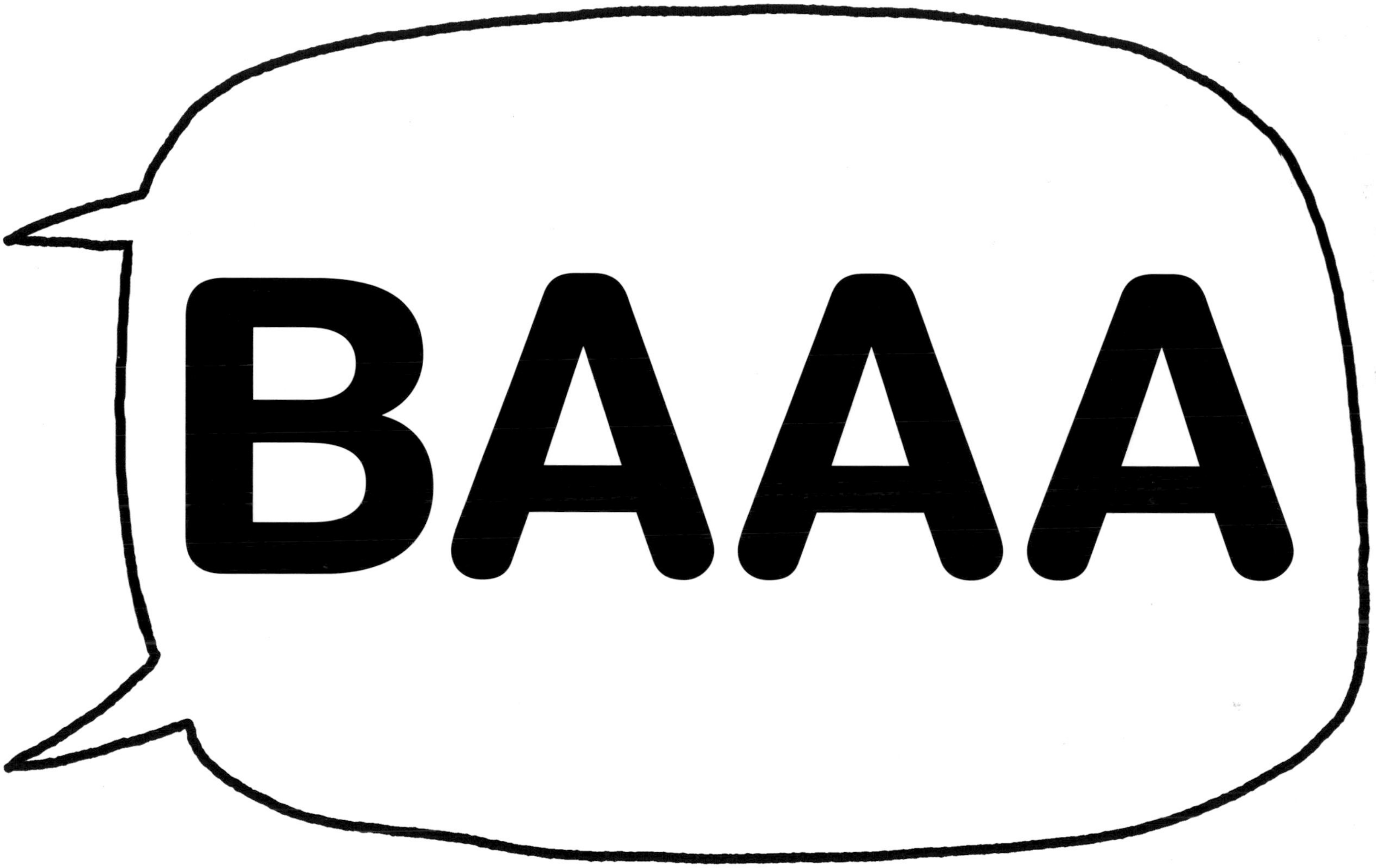
BAAA

"Why are you saying baa?" asked Lamb.

"You're not sheep."

"We like baa," said Calf.

"Can you make other noises?" asked Lamb.

"We could try oink," said Little Rabbit.

"I like oink," said Calf.

"Me too," said Lamb.

And they "oinked" as loud as they could.

"Why are you saying oink?" asked Piglet.

"You're not pigs."

"We like oink," said Lamb.

"Do you know any other noises?" asked Piglet.

"Hee-haw is a good one," said Little Rabbit.

"I like hee-haw," said Lamb.

"Me too," said Piglet.

"Cool," said Calf.

And they "hee-hawed" as hard as they could.

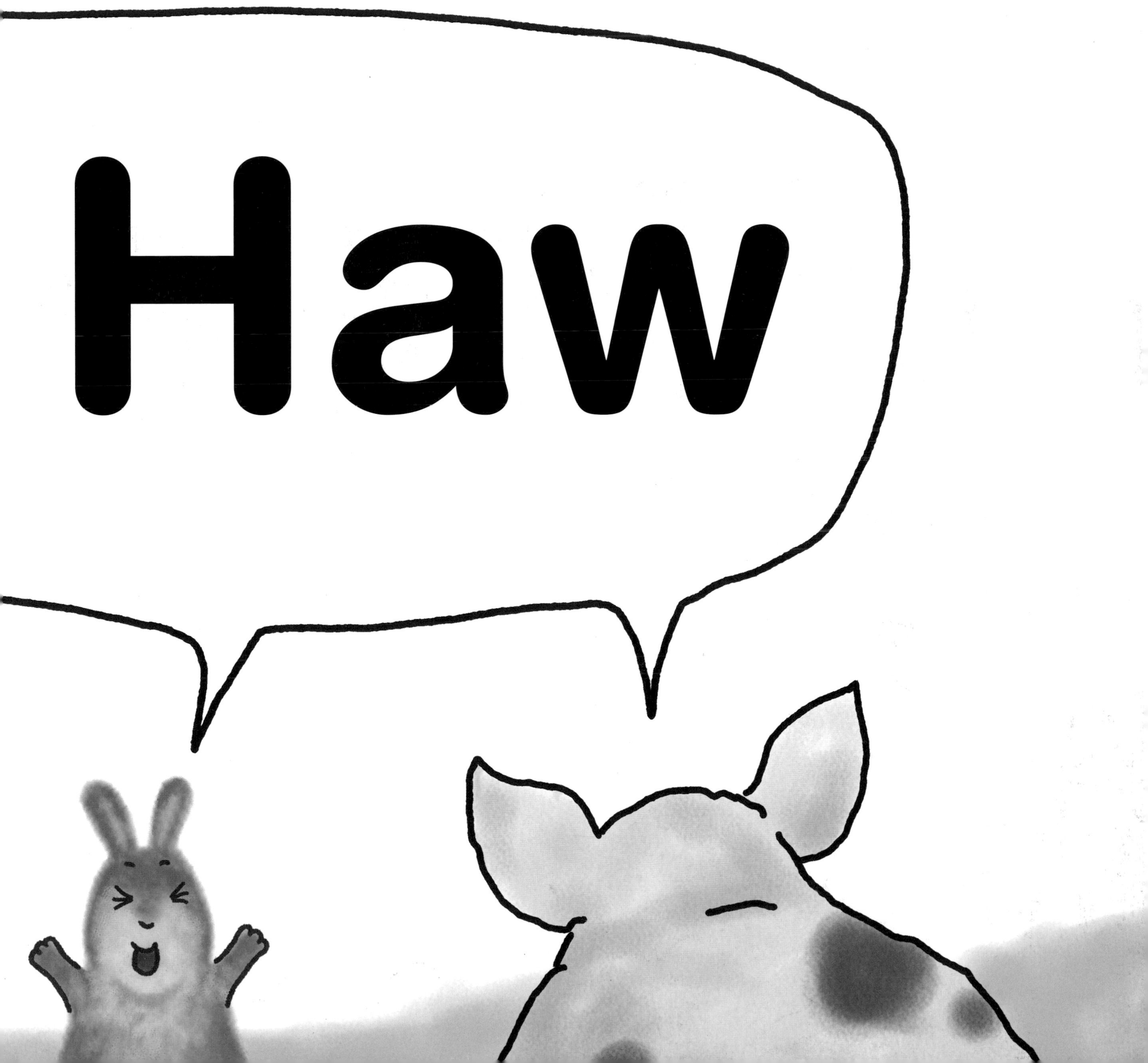
Haw

"Why are you saying hee-haw?" asked Baby Donkey.
"You're not donkeys."

"We like hee-haw," said Piglet.
"Can you make other noises?"
asked Baby Donkey.

"I like quack," said Piglet.

"Me too," said Lamb.

"Good one," said Calf.

"Okay," said Baby Donkey.

"Let's do it," said Little Rabbit.

And they "quacked"
as loud as they could.

"Why are you all saying quack?"
asked Duckling. "You're not ducks."
"I like quack," said Baby Donkey.

"So do I," said Piglet.

"Me too," said Lamb and Calf.

"Me too," said Little Rabbit.

"Is it your favourite animal sound?" asked Duckling.

"Other noises are fun," said Calf,
"but I like moo best. After all,
I am a baby cow."

"I like baa best," said Lamb.
"But then, I am a baby sheep."

"For a baby pig like me," said Piglet,
"there is no better noise than oink."

"Nothing beats quack," said Duckling.

"My favourite is hee-haw," said Baby Donkey.

"I have a favourite," said Little Rabbit . . .

Other Boxer Books paperbacks

I'm not Cute!: **Jonathan Allen**

"I'm NOT cute!" said Baby Owl.
"And I am not small."
A perfect bedtime read - and a real hoot.
Shortlisted - Pre-School Award 2006
BOOK TRUST EARLY YEARS AWARDS
ISBN 13: 978-0-954737-38-2

I'm not Scared: **Jonathan Allen**

"I'm NOT scared!" said Baby Owl.
"And I should be out in the woods at night.
It's what owls DO!"
Baby Owl decides to explore the woods
at night with hilarious consequences in
another perfect bedtime read.
ISBN 13: 978-1-905417-28-5

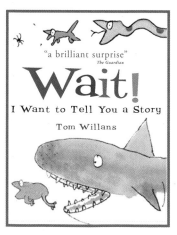

Wait! I Want to Tell You a Story: **Tom Willans**

"I'm going to eat you, little muskrat,"
said the tiger.
"Wait!" said the muskrat.
"I want to tell you a story."
'a brilliant surprise'
THE GUARDIAN
ISBN 13: 978-0-954737-37-5